Henry Holt and Company, LLC
Publishers since 1866
175 Fifth Avenue
New York, New York 10010
mackids.com

Henry Holt® is a registered trademark of Henry Holt and Company, LLC.
Copyright © 2009 by Nancy Coffelt
All rights reserved.

Library of Congress Cataloging-in-Publication Data
Coffelt, Nancy.
Big, bigger, biggest! / Nancy Coffelt.—1st ed.
p.   cm.
ISBN 978-0-8050-8089-6
1. English language—Comparison—Juvenile literature. 2. English language—Synonyms and antonyms—
Juvenile literature. 3. English language—Adjective—Juvenile literature. I. Title.
PE1241.C64 2009   423'.1—dc22   2008018335

First Edition—2009 / Designed by Elizabeth Tardiff
The artist used acrylic paint on canvas to create the illustrations for this book.
Printed in China by RR Donnelley Asia Printing Solutions Ltd., Dongguan City, Guangdong Province.

5 7 9 10 8 6

Big, Bigger, BIGGEST!

Nancy Coffelt

Christy Ottaviano Books

Henry Holt and Company

New York

For the "fourables"
—N. C.

I'm big.

I'm large. I'm huge. I'm jumbo.

I'm bigger.

I'm gigantic.
I'm immense.
I'm enormous.

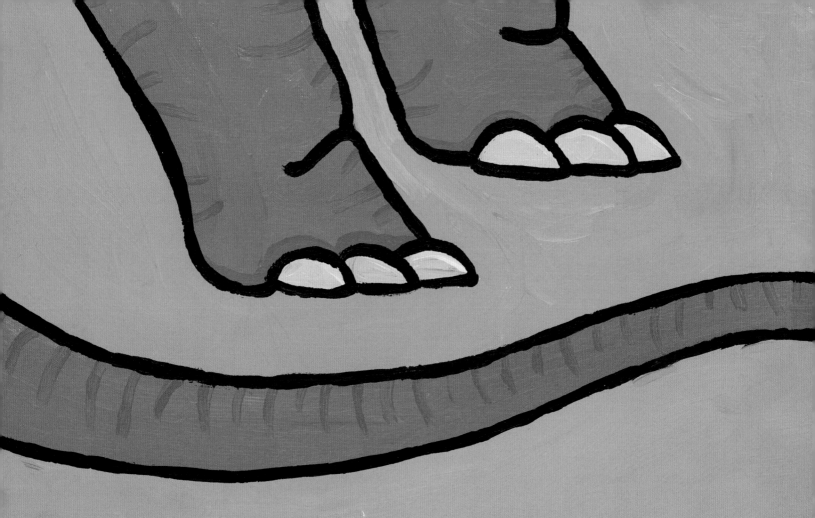

I'm biggest!

I'm mammoth.
I'm humongous.
I'm colossal!

I'm small.

I'm little. I'm teensy. I'm wee.

I'm smaller.

I'm petite.
I'm tiny.
I'm itty-bitty.

I'm smallest!

I'm miniature.
I'm minuscule.
I'm microscopic!

I'm fast.

I'm quick. I'm hasty. I'm speedy.

I'm faster.

I'm nimble. I'm rapid. I'm swift.

I'm fastest!

I'm fleet. I'm meteoric.
I'm hypersonic!

I'm slow.

I'm plodding.
I'm languid.
I'm ponderous.

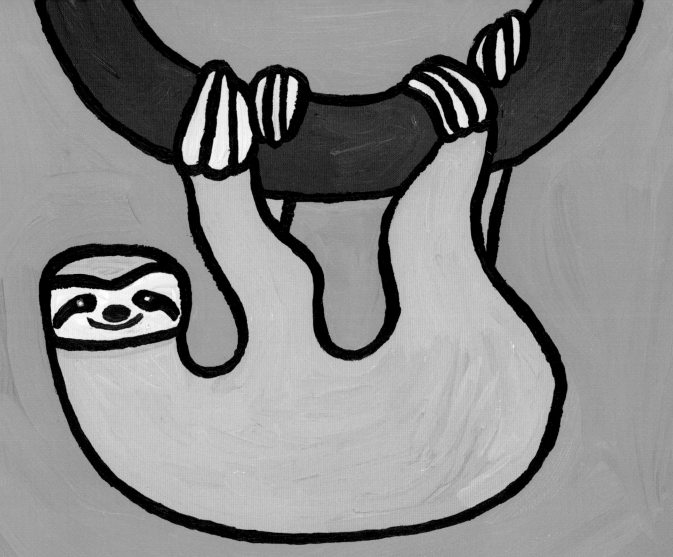

I'm slower.

I'm poky.
I'm laggard.
I'm slothful.

I'm slowest!

I'm sluggish.
I'm lethargic.
I'm lackadaisical!

I'm hungry.

I'm empty. I'm starving.
I'm famished.

I'm hungrier.

I'm piggish. I'm hoggish.
I'm ravenous.

I'm hungriest!

I'm insatiable.
I'm voracious.
I'm rapacious!

I'm slimy.

I'm damp. I'm dank. I'm moist.

I'm slimier.

I'm viscous.
I'm slippery.
I'm slick.

I'm slimiest!

I'm clammy.
I'm oozy.
I'm gooey!

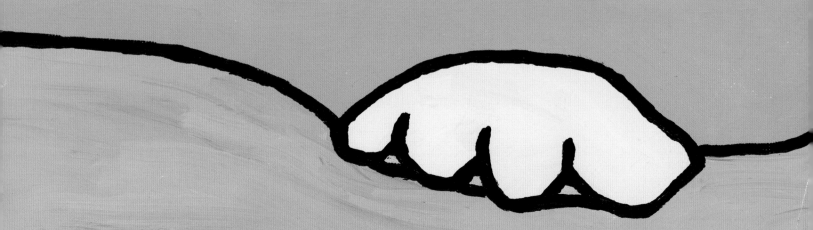

I'm sleepy.

I'm tired. I'm drowsy. I'm spent.

I'm sleepier.

I'm pooped.
I'm droopy.
I'm slumberous.

I'm sleepiest!

I'm exhausted.
I'm somnolent.
I'm dreamy...

Good night!

This book is over.

Finished. Ended.
Completed. Concluded.
Through.
Done.